P9-CMK-731

For Ben, Sophie, Cooper, Hannah, and all
the others who grow with the special love
that knows no borders.

Special thanks to Lisa Coker, Cameron
and Hannah's mom, and Namyi Min,
Spence-Chapin Services.

Copyright © 2009 by Yumi Heo ✳ All rights reserved. ✳ Published in the United States by Schwartz & Wade Books,
an imprint of Random House Children's Books, a division of Random House, Inc., New York ✳ Schwartz & Wade Books and
the colophon are trademarks of Random House, Inc. ✳ Visit us on the Web! www.randomhouse.com/kids
Educators and librarians, for a variety of teaching tools, visit us at www.randomhouse.com/teachers

Library of Congress Cataloging-in-Publication Data ✳ Heo, Yumi. ✳ Ten days and nine nights / Yumi Heo. — 1st ed. ✳ p. cm.
Summary: A young girl eagerly awaits the arrival of her newly-adopted sister from Korea, while her whole family prepares.
ISBN 978-0-375-84718-9 (hardcover) — ISBN 978-0-375-94715-5 (Gibraltar lib. bdg.)
[1. Adoption—Fiction. 2. Sisters—Fiction. 3. Family life—Fiction. 4. Korean Americans—Fiction.] ✳ I. Title.
PZ7.H4117Ten 2009 ✳ [E]—dc22 ✳ 2007044073

The text of this book is set in Tyrnavia.
The illustrations are rendered in oil, pencil, and collage on 140-pound Fabriano paper.
MANUFACTURED IN MALAYSIA ✳ 10 9 8 7 6 5 4 3 2 1 ✳ May 2009 ✳ First Edition
Random House Children's Books supports the First Amendment and celebrates the right to read.

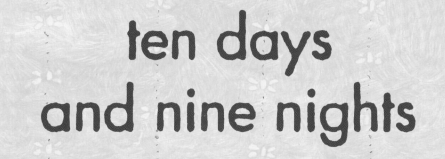

ten days
and nine nights

an adoption story by
yumi heo

HA CASS COUNTY PUBLIC LIBRARY
400 E. MECHANIC
HARRISONVILLE, MO 64701

0 0022 0364814 8

schwartz & wade books · new york

I mark a circle on the calendar.

I have ten days
and nine nights.

May

1	2	3	4	5	6
7	8	9	⑩	11	12	13
14	15	16	17	18	19	20
21	22	23	24	25	26	27
28	29		31			

Daddy and I say goodbye to Mommy.

I have nine days
and eight nights.

I make a drawing of my kitty and cut
a heart shape from red paper.

I have eight days
and seven nights.

Grandpa redecorates my room.

I have seven days
and six nights.

I practice.

I have six days
and five nights.

Daddy buys some new furniture.

I have five days
and four nights.

I wash my old teddy bear.

I have four days
and three nights.

Grandma makes a little pink dress.

I have three days
and two nights.

I tell Molly.

I have two days
and one night.

Daddy puts the CLOSED sign
on his dry cleaning store.

I have only
one day!

At last!

I have no days
and no nights.

I have a new baby sister.

author's note

The first time I met a child who had been adopted from Korea—where I was born and lived until I was twenty-four years old—was eighteen years ago on a ski trip to Massachusetts. I was cautiously learning to step with my long skis, and he was my teenage instructor. It was strange to see someone from my country who was so adept at a Western sport, but it also made me feel proud of him. He had come such a long way, without his birth parents, and was thriving. Over the years, as I settled in the suburbs and raised my own family, I ran into Asian—and particularly Korean—adoptees more often. When my son was in preschool, the parents of his best friend, Cameron, adopted a little girl, Hannah, from Korea. My neighbor's good friends' children were adopted from Korea; now they are in college. My friends Shirley and David adopted their three children from Cambodia. For years, Ben, their first child, thought babies came from airplanes! As a Korean who adopted the United States as my home, I've always felt a kinship with these children. I wanted to create a story especially for them and their new families.

a few facts: The number of children adopted from other countries increases every year in the United States. In Korea, before children are adopted they are usually placed in foster homes. Most countries that allow international adoption place children in group homes or orphanages, but there are some that use foster homes as well.

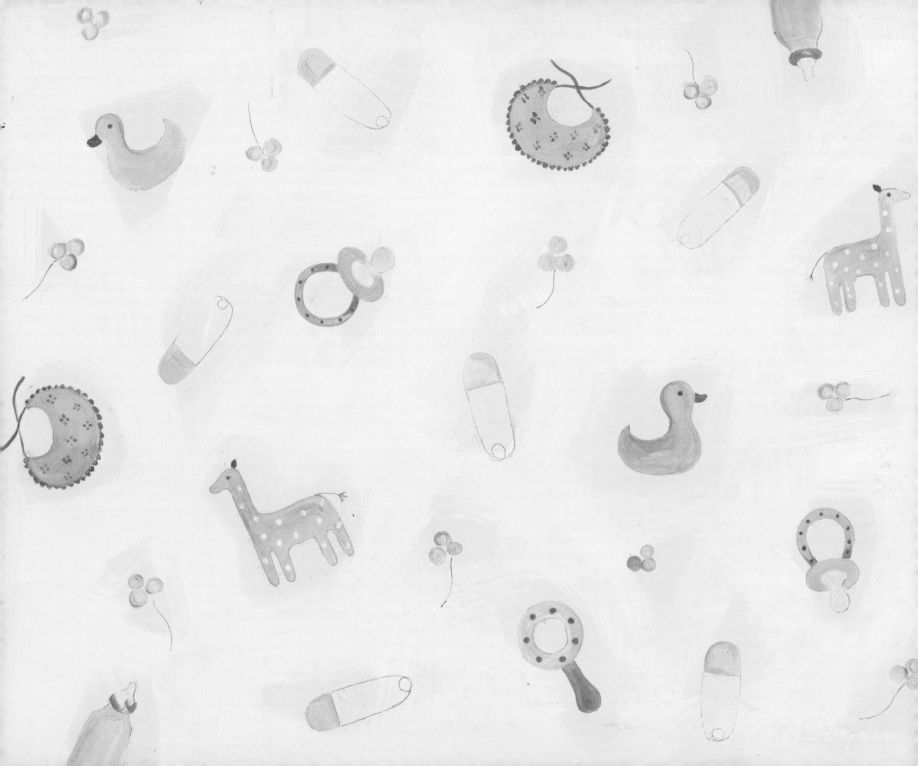